All The Better To See You With!

Margaret Wild

Illustrated by Pat Reynolds

ALBERT WHITMAN & COMPANY, MORTON GROVE, ILLINOIS

K ate has four brothers and sisters. They are big and noisy and feisty, even the baby.

Kate is small and quiet and "no trouble at all," her mother always says with a thankful smile.

It's easy not to take much notice of Kate. Sometimes her family even forgets she's there.

But now and again, when Dad is looking after the other children, Mom makes a special fuss over Kate. She washes her long, brown hair and blows it dry. Then she brushes it one hundred times to make it shine.

And all the while, she and Kate play the game they've been playing since Kate was a baby.

"What big, white teeth you have!" says Mom.

"All the better to nibble you with, my dear," says Kate.

"What a big, smiley mouth you have!" says Mom.

"All the better to kiss you with, my dear," says Kate.

"What big, brown eyes you have!" says Mom.

"All the better to see you with, my dear," says Kate.

But, although Kate doesn't know it, she really can't see very well at all. When she's sitting close to Mom, she can see the little bump on her nose and the funny freckle on her cheek.

But when Mom's walking home from the bus stop, all Kate can see is a splash of red, a splash of blue, and a splash of brown. She knows it's Mom, because those are her clothes, but her face is just a blurry blob.

Kate is used to blurry blobs and splashes of color.

When she's in the city, this is what she sees:

When she's in the country, this is what she sees:

When she's at the top of the slide, this is what she sees:

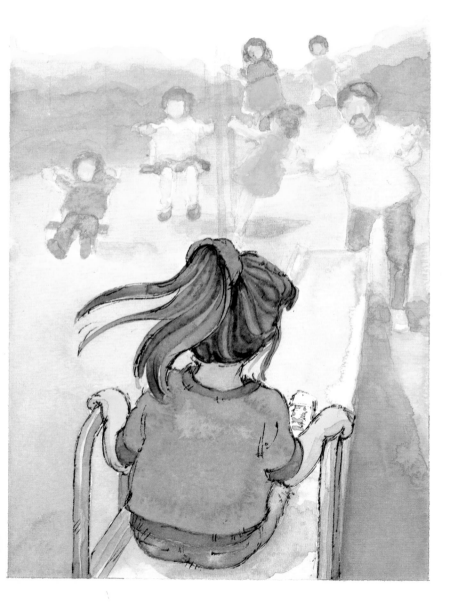

And when she stares out of her bedroom window, this is what she sees:

If Kate were big and noisy and feisty, perhaps someone would say, "Hey, Kate, why are you sitting so close to the TV?" Or, "Hey, Kate, why didn't you wave back to Mrs. Battiwalla?" Or, "Hey, Kate, why do you always fall asleep at the movies?"

But Kate is small and quiet and no trouble at all. She doesn't know what other people can see, and no one thinks to ask her what *she* sees.

One Sunday, at the beach, while the other children are making sandcastles, Kate goes off on her own to paddle. When she comes out of the water, she can't see her family anywhere.

She runs up and down the beach, peering this way and that.

At last, her mother catches her by the arm, takes her back to the umbrella, and wraps a towel around her.

"What was the matter?" Mom asks. "You ran right past us twice."

Kate shivers. "I couldn't see you. All the umbrellas and the people look the same."

"What?" says her mother. Then she says very carefully,
"Can you see the ship over there, Kate, on the horizon?"
"What ship?" says Kate. "What horizon?"

Dad says slowly, as if he's thinking, "Can you see the
seagulls over there, Kate, on the pier?"
"What seagulls?" says Kate. "What pier?"

Mom and Dad stare across the sand at their noisy, feisty family. Then they put their arms around Kate.

"My little Kate," says Mom. "I'm so very sorry."

"We should have noticed ages ago that you can't see well," says Dad. "You must be nearsighted. That means you can't see faraway things clearly. You need glasses, Kate."

"Glasses!" says Kate. "For me?" And she feels a flutter of excitement in her stomach.

So, Mom makes an appointment and takes Kate to the eye doctor to have her eyes tested.

Then Kate chooses the frames she likes.

"They make you look older," says Mom, "and very important."

Kate has to wait a week for her glasses to be made. It's a long, long week.

"You're lucky," says her sister. "I wish I was getting glasses."

"Gla, gla, gla!" shouts the baby, climbing on Kate's knee.

She hugs him, her eyes shining, and thinks, "Soon I'll be able to see, really see! What will it be like?"

A week later, Kate puts her new glasses on her nose.
Her heart thumps. She shuts her eyes, then opens them.

Now, when Kate's in the city, this is what she sees:

When she's in the country, this is what she sees:

When she's at the top of the slide,
this is what she sees:

And when she stares out of her
bedroom window, this is what she sees:

And now and again, when Mom brushes her hair and says, "What big, shining glasses you have!" Kate laughs and says, "All the better to see you and Dad and the kids and the baby and *everything* with, my dear!"

For Karen and Danny. M.W.

Published in 1993 by Albert Whitman & Company,
6340 Oakton St., Morton Grove, Illinois 60053-2723.
Published simultaneously in Canada by
General Publishing, Limited, Toronto.
First published in 1992 by Allen & Unwin Pty Ltd,
St Leonards, NSW 2065, Australia (A Little Ark Book).
This book is copyright under the Berne Convention.
No reproduction without permission.
All rights reserved.
Printed and bound in the U.S.A.
10 9 8 7 6 5 4 3 2 1

Designed by Sandra Nobes.
The typeface is Goudy.

Library of Congress Cataloging-in-Publication Data

Wild, Margaret, 1948-
   All the better to see you with!/Margaret Wild; illustrated by
Pat Reynolds.
      p.   cm.
   Summary: Because Kate is the quiet one compared to her four
noisy brothers and sisters, her parents are slow to notice that
she is nearsighted and needs glasses.
   ISBN 0-8075-0284-7
   [1. Eyeglasses—Fiction.] I. Reynolds, Pat, ill. II. Title.
PZ7.W64574A1   1993   92-39127
[E]—dc20   CIP
                                                 AC